Elisa Michaels, Bigger & Better

By Johanna Hurwitz

MAKE ROOM FOR ELISA

MUCH ADO ABOUT ALDO

NEW NEIGHBORS FOR NORA

NEW SHOES FOR SILVIA

NORA AND
MRS. MIND-YOUR-OWN-BUSINESS

ONCE I WAS A PLUM TREE

ONE SMALL DOG

OZZIE ON HIS OWN

THE RABBI'S GIRLS

RIP-ROARING RUSSELL

ROZ AND OZZIE

RUSSELL AND ELISA

RUSSELL RIDES AGAIN

RUSSELL SPROUTS

RUSSELL'S SECRET

SCHOOL'S OUT

SCHOOL SPIRIT

SPRING BREAK

STARTING SCHOOL

SUMMER WITH ELISA

SUPERDUPER TEDDY

TEACHER'S PET

TOUGH-LUCK KAREN

THE UP & DOWN SPRING

A WORD TO THE WISE: AND OTHER PROVERBS

YELLOW BLUE JAY

Johanna Hurwitz

Elisa Michaels, Bigger & Better

illustrated by Debbie Tilley

HarperCollinsPublishers

Library of Congress Cataloging-in-Publication Data
Hurwitz, Johanna.
  Elisa Michaels, bigger & better / Johanna Hurwitz ; illustrated by Debbie
Tilley.
     p.   cm.
  Contents: Breakfast with Grandma—The baby-sitter—What Marshall
needed—Chocolate all day long—Marshall makes mischief—From Riverside
to Lakeside.
  ISBN 0-06-009601-2—ISBN 0-06-009602-0 (lib. bdg.)
  1. Children's stories, American. [1. Short stories.] I. Tilley, Debbie, ill. II. Title.
PZ7.H9574 En 2003   2002151928
[Fic]—dc21   CIP
                                                                         AC

3 4 5 6 7 8 9 10
❖
First Edition

For Rosemary Brosnan—
A good editor is better
than chocolate.

Contents

Breakfast with Grandma

It was the second week of September, and Elisa Michaels was sitting at the kitchen table doing her homework. She was writing a report for her second-grade class. Whenever she came to a hard word, she asked her mother for help.

There are five people in my family, she wrote. *I have a big brother and a little brother. My big brother is named Russell. He is eleven years old. My little brother is Marshall. I call him Marshie because he's soft like a marshmallow. He is two years old. I have a mommy and a daddy. I don't know how old they are.*

Elisa put down her pencil. "Mommy, how old are you?" she asked.

"Why do you want to know that?" Mrs. Michaels inquired. She was standing nearby ironing.

"I need the information for my report."

"Are you writing a report about me?" Mrs. Michaels asked, sounding surprised.

"I am writing about our whole family."

"You can skip the part about my age," Mrs. Michaels told her. "Tell about your brothers and yourself."

Elisa looked at Marshall, who was sitting on the kitchen floor with his pacifier in his mouth and happily rolling a ball toward the wall. When the ball returned to him, he rolled it again. Elisa liked to play with him.

Everyone who saw Marshall commented on what a good toddler he was and how well he could entertain himself. Elisa didn't want to write about that. And she didn't want to write about Russell, who was growing so big that soon he would be as tall as their mother. Sometimes Russell teased Elisa. Sometimes he was mean. Mostly, though, she thought he was a good brother. She could say that, but she didn't want to.

Elisa pushed her eyeglasses up on her nose. She could say that she wore glasses, but everyone who saw her would already know that. She could say that she was seven years old, but everyone in second grade was seven or going to have a birthday very soon. She could say that she'd lost her two top teeth, but everyone could see that, too. Then she got another idea.

I have two cousins. One is Howie. He is almost the same age as Russell. The other cousin is Artie. He is nine years old. Their real names are Howard and Arthur. No one ever calls them that. I have three grandparents. I don't see them very much, because they live far away. I am glad my mommy and daddy don't live far away.

Mrs. Michaels looked over Elisa's shoulder. "Very good," she said. "How much did the teacher say you had to write?"

"One page," said Elisa. The words she had written almost covered the paper in front of her.

"I am going to copy it over to make it neater," she told her mother. "If I write a little bigger, it will be just right."

"You didn't tell anything about your grandparents. How they come to visit, the gifts they send even when it isn't your birthday, the special things you do with them."

"I wrote enough," said Elisa. "Writing is hard work."

"Welcome to the real world," said Russell,

coming into the kitchen. "And if you think second grade is hard, wait until you get as old as I am."

"Will you help me with my homework when I'm in sixth grade?" Elisa asked.

"Fat chance," said Russell. "When you're in sixth grade, I'll be in high school. I'm not going to have time to help you."

"I wouldn't worry about sixth grade now," said Mrs. Michaels as she folded up the ironing board and put it away. "And you're doing just fine in second grade."

"Anyhow, what's for supper?" asked Russell. "I'm starving."

"Look," said his mother, pulling a pan out of the refrigerator.

"Lasagna! My favorite," Russell shouted when he saw it. "Hurry and put it in the oven."

"Who wants to help me cut up the vegetables for a salad?" she asked.

"Not me," said Russell. "I've got tons of

homework. I just came to check on supper."

"I'll help," said Elisa. "I can copy my homework later."

"Then put your papers away and wash your hands," said her mother.

As Elisa tore the lettuce leaves into small pieces, she said, "I wish Grandma could come and visit. I haven't seen her in a long, long, long time."

Grandma was what Elisa called her mother's mother. *Nana* was what she called her other grandmother.

"Grandma is planning to come here in April," Mrs. Michaels said.

Elisa stopped tearing the lettuce leaves and counted out the months on her fingers: "Seven months," she said. "That's too long to wait."

"Seven months is a long time," agreed Mrs. Michaels.

Marshall pulled his pacifier out of his

mouth. "One-four-five-seven-eight-nine-ten," he called out before sticking the pacifier back inside his mouth.

"I miss her," said Elisa. "We always have good talks together. She tells me about when she was a little girl, and she tells me about when you were a little girl."

"I know," her mother said. "And I'm sure she misses you and those long conversations that you have, too."

"I wish she would come right now," Elisa complained.

"She'll come, but you just have to be patient."

Elisa sniffed back a tear.

Suddenly her mother laughed. "I have an idea," she said. "How would you like to have breakfast with Grandma on Saturday?"

"Could I?" asked Elisa eagerly.

"I think so. I have a plan," said Mrs. Michaels. "I'll try and work it out so that just you and Grandma have breakfast together on Saturday morning."

"But it won't be April on Saturday. Will she be here anyway?" asked Elisa.

"That's part of my plan. If it all works out, you and Grandma will have breakfast together."

"No one else? Not you? Not Russell? Not Daddy? Or Marshall?"

"No one else. Just you and Grandma."

"Will it be in a restaurant?" asked Elisa, remembering one visit when she and her grandmother had gone off together for breakfast by themselves.

"You'll see," said Mrs. Michaels, smiling.

Sure enough, on Saturday morning, Elisa had breakfast with Grandma and no one else was there.

Elisa was wearing her blue velvet party dress and feeling very special.

"What are you going to eat this morning?" Grandma asked Elisa.

"Pancakes. It's my favorite breakfast."

"Mine too," said Grandma.

"Is that what you're having?" asked Elisa.

"No." Grandma sighed. "I'm having a bowl of oatmeal."

"Well, if you like pancakes best, why don't you eat them, like me?" asked Elisa. "I thought you could eat whatever you want when you're a grown-up."

"I used to think so too when I was your age. But now I know otherwise. Besides, oatmeal is better for a woman of my age."

"What is your age?" asked Elisa.

"Two hundred and seventeen," said Grandma.

"Really?"

"No. Not really. But I'm very old. And eating oatmeal will help me get even older."

"Oh."

"Now tell me all about school," Grandma said, changing the subject. "Do you like first grade?"

"Oh, Grandma. You're joking. You know I finished first grade. I'm in second grade now."

"My goodness, you're growing old, too. Soon you'll be as old as I am."

"Grandma, I'll never grow as old as you. I can't even grow as old as Russell. As soon as I grow older, he grows older, too. He's always going to be my big brother. And you're always going to be my old grandmother."

"That's good. I love being your grandmother," Grandma said.

Elisa chewed on a pancake. She swallowed, and a piece of pancake went down the wrong way. It made her cough.

"Watch it," said Grandma. "I think you're eating too fast. Take a big swallow of milk and wash that down."

Elisa gulped down some milk and felt better.

"Did my mommy like pancakes when she was my age?" asked Elisa.

"She sure did. Sometimes I made them in shapes."

"Shapes?"

"Like animals or letters of the alphabet."

"That sounds like fun."

"It *was* fun. But you know what?"

"What?" asked Elisa.

"The shapes tasted exactly the same as the little round pancakes that you're eating now."

"I can cut my pancakes into shapes," Elisa said. She tried to do it, but it was sticky work because of the syrup.

"I wouldn't bother with making shapes. Just enjoy the taste. That's what's important," said Grandma. "And they all get mashed up when you chew them anyway. Tell me, did anything special happen in school this week?"

"My teacher was wearing shoes with high heels. Then at lunchtime, one of her heels broke off. So she had to walk around without any shoes at all. I never saw a teacher without shoes before."

"I never saw a teacher without shoes either," said Grandma.

"Oh, I feel so full," said Elisa. "I ate all four pancakes on my plate. That's the most I ever had."

"No wonder you're full," said Grandma.

"Russell once ate seven pancakes," said Elisa. "I could never do that."

"You don't have to try to do the things Russell does."

"Oh, yes," Elisa insisted. "Otherwise I'll always be a little girl. I want to do everything he does."

"I know," Grandma said. "I heard all

about how you climbed a tree last summer and then had trouble getting down. And the only reason you climbed up was because Russell had done the same thing."

"But it was fun," said Elisa, remembering that experience.

"It may be fun now, but I don't think it was so much fun when you were up in the tree," said Grandma.

"It was a little fun," said Elisa.

"Elisa, you do Elisa things. Russell will do Russell things. And I'll do Grandma things."

"Does that mean you won't climb a tree?" asked Elisa.

"It certainly does. And it means that I have to go to the beauty parlor now because I have an appointment to get my hair cut."

"I think you look pretty just the way you are," said Elisa.

"And I always think you're pretty too,"

said Grandma. "But I'm still going to the beauty parlor. Let's plan to have breakfast together again in a couple of weeks. Okay?"

"Okay," said Elisa. "Maybe I can get Mommy to make my pancakes in shapes next time."

"Next time I'm going to remember to have raisins nearby to put on my oatmeal," said Grandma. "Have a good week, sweetheart, and give Russell and Marshall a hug from me."

"I'll hug Marshie, but I don't think Russell will want one. Maybe if you gave it to him, but he won't let me give it."

"That's all right. Tell him I sent a hug."

"Okay."

"Bye-bye, sweetie. Remember that I love you."

"Bye, Grandma. I love you too."

"I love you three," said Grandma.

There was a click on the telephone and

then silence. Elisa listened to quiet. It was funny to be sitting in the dining room holding onto a sticky telephone. She'd never eaten and spoken on the phone at the same time. Maybe she should write her report all over again. She could tell about how she'd had breakfast with her grandmother, even if they couldn't see each other because her grandmother was far away in Lakeside, Florida. It had been very special. And they were going to do it again very soon.

The Baby-sitter

The Michaels family lived on the fourth floor of their apartment building in New York City, not far from Riverside Drive. The building had eight stories, and Elisa and Russell knew people on each one. Their oldest friend was Mrs. Wurmbrand, whose apartment was on the top floor. She was over ninety years old. The children called her Mrs. W. for short.

On the seventh floor lived Nora and

Teddy. Nora was older than her brother. She was fourteen and sometimes she baby-sat when Mr. and Mrs. Michaels went out for the evening.

"I don't need a baby-sitter," Russell always said. "Boys my age can take care of themselves."

"Well, someone has to be here to keep an eye on Marshall and Elisa," their mother pointed out.

Teddy was two years younger than Nora. He was almost old enough to baby-sit, too.

"Teddy is my friend. He can't be my baby-sitter," said Russell.

"You're right," his mother agreed. "I'm afraid if Teddy ever came to baby-sit, the two of you would be so busy playing together you wouldn't pay any attention to Marshall."

On the fourth floor, across the hall from the Michaels family, lived Eugene Spencer Eastman and his parents. Eugene Spencer was an only child.

"He's not only a child," insisted Elisa. "He's practically grown up." Eugene Spencer was older than Nora. He was fifteen.

"An only child means that he doesn't have any brothers or sisters," Russell explained. "Sometimes I wish I was an only child," he added.

"You do?" asked Elisa. How could her brother say a thing like that?

"He's only teasing," their mother said. "Russell would be very lonely without you and Marshall around."

"That's right," Elisa said. She knew she'd be very lonely without her two brothers. She could hardly remember back to the time when she had only one brother, before Marshall was born.

One Saturday afternoon, Mrs. Michaels received a phone call from Nora and Teddy's mother. It seemed that Nora wasn't feeling well. "Her mother thinks she's come down with the flu," said Mrs. Michaels.

"Oh, poor Nora," said Elisa. "I'm glad I'm not sick."

"I'm sure it's nothing serious," said Mrs. Michaels. "But remember, Nora was going to stay with you children this evening when your father and I go to the theater."

"That's okay. I'll be in charge," said Russell, who had just walked into the room and overheard the end of the conversation.

"I'm afraid you're too young to be in charge of two small children and yourself," said his mother.

"I'm not small," protested Elisa.

"Yes, you are," said Russell. "But I could still be the baby-sitter."

"Marshall is small. I'm big. Seven isn't a baby. Baby-sitters are for babies like Marshall," Elisa said.

"Well, big or small, someone has to be

here this evening if your father and I are going out," said Mrs. Michaels. She picked up her address book and began flipping the pages. "There must be someone I can call," she muttered aloud.

In the end, the person she called was Eugene Spencer. It seemed funny to Elisa to watch her mother speaking on the phone with their neighbor when all she had to do was open the door to the apartment and ring the doorbell across the hall.

"All right. It's settled," said Mrs. Michaels, beaming when she got off the phone. "Eugene Spencer has never baby-sat before, but I told him it won't be any problem. Every baby-sitter has a first time, and you'll be his first experience."

"Well he's not baby-sitting for me," said Russell. "I told you I don't need a sitter. He can just pretend that I'm not here. And I'll pretend that he's not here too."

"But I told him that you and Elisa would help him out if he ran into any problems," she said, looking at her two older children.

"Well, if we help, we should get paid," said Russell. "Baby-sitters always get paid."

"We'll see about that," said Mrs. Michaels, without making any commitment.

"I'll help him for free," offered Elisa. She was sorry that Nora wasn't coming to their house that evening, but she thought it would be interesting to have Eugene Spencer there. At fifteen he was too old to play with Russell, and although she knew her parents considered him to still be young, she thought of him as almost an adult. After all, he went to high school and he was as tall as her father.

Supper was a little earlier than usual so that Marshall could be bathed and in his crib before Eugene Spencer arrived.

"It never fails." Mrs. Michaels sighed as

she buttoned her dress. "Most nights Marshall is sound asleep by seven o'clock. But here it is seven fifteen and he's still wide awake."

Elisa could hear Marshall talking to himself in his bedroom. His vocabulary was growing every day and he often sang the songs that he'd heard on his kiddy television programs.

The doorbell rang. It was Eugene Spencer. "Here I am," he announced.

"We can see that," said Elisa.

Russell forgot that he was going to ignore their baby-sitter. "Hi," he greeted him. "Do you know how to play chess?"

Eugene Spencer's eyes lit up. "I don't know anything about baby-sitting," he told Russell, "but I'm great at chess. I'm on the chess team at school. I'll probably beat you in half a dozen moves."

"No you won't," said Russell. "I'm pretty

good. In fact, I'm very good." He went to his bedroom and returned holding a chessboard and a box of pieces.

"Since it's the weekend, Russell can stay up until ten P.M.," Mrs. Michaels instructed Eugene Spencer.

"Mom," protested Russell.

She ignored him. "And Elisa should be in bed by nine thirty," she continued.

"Okay," said their baby-sitter, looking up from the dining table, where he was setting up the chess pieces. He took a black and a white pawn and put them behind his back, one piece in each hand. "What do you pick?" he asked Russell.

"Left," said Russell.

Eugene Spencer opened his left hand.

"Yay. I got white. I go first," Russell said, turning his attention to the chessboard.

Elisa sighed. Recently she had learned how to play chess, too. But it was very rare

that Russell agreed to play a game with her. "It's no challenge," he told her whenever she asked. She didn't think Eugene Spencer would want to play with her either.

"Good-night, kids," said Mr. Michaels. "Be good."

"There's a box of cookies on the kitchen counter," said Mrs. Michaels. "Help yourselves to milk or juice from the fridge." She paused a moment. "I think three cookies each is plenty for Russell and Elisa. But you can have as many as you want," she told Eugene Spencer.

"No fair," said Russell, moving one of his pieces on the chessboard.

Eugene Spencer nodded, but whether it was about the cookies or Russell's chess move, Elisa didn't know.

"'Night," she said, giving each of her parents a hug. She sniffed the perfume her mother was wearing. It smelled good.

"See you in the morning, honey," called Mrs. Michaels as the door closed behind her.

Elisa went to get one of her new library books. As she passed Marshall's room, she could hear that he was still awake. "Ma, ma, ma, ma," he was calling out. It meant he wanted his mother to come to him, but Elisa knew that most nights her mother didn't go. She let him talk and sing and call until he tired himself out and fell asleep.

Elisa took her book and went to sit in the living room. She would wait and eat her three cookies later, together with Russell and Eugene Spencer. She could hear the two older boys talking together.

"Touch move," Eugene Spencer called out. "Your hand touched that piece. You have to move it."

"I was just straightening it out on the board," Russell protested.

"No way," said his opponent.

"Mamamama," Marshall called from his crib. There was an urgency to his tone that hadn't been there before.

Elisa got up and walked to the door of Marshall's room. Very quietly she turned the door handle. She sniffed the air. Then she walked into the living room.

"Marshall has a poopy diaper," she announced.

Eugene Spencer looked up. "Does that mean what I think?" he asked.

"Yeah," said Russell.

"Well, what do you do about it?"

"I don't do anything," said Russell. "You're the baby-sitter. You do something."

"I don't know how," said Eugene Spencer. "You better do it to show me how."

"No way," said Russell. "It'll spoil my appetite for the cookies."

"I can do it," said Elisa. Her mother never let her change the baby's diaper, but she'd watched about a hundred times, so she knew exactly how it was done.

"Okay," said Eugene Spencer.

Elisa walked toward Marshall's room. She had expected Eugene Spencer to come along and watch her. He seemed to have forgotten that he'd asked Russell to show him how. How was he ever going to learn if he didn't watch her? She opened the door and turned the light on. "Hi, Marshie," she said, breathing through her mouth.

Marshall was standing up in his crib, squinting from the bright light. "Leesie, Leesie," he called out in delight. It was the way he pronounced his sister's name these days.

Elisa knew she wasn't tall enough to change Marshall's diaper while he was inside the crib. And she also wasn't strong enough to take him out. So she went to the drawer where her mother stored the disposable diapers and took one. She also grabbed a couple of wipes. Then, holding these things, she climbed up and inside the crib.

"Leesie, Leesie," Marshall crooned happily.

"Lie down, Marshie," Elisa instructed her brother. "I'm going to change your diaper."

Sometimes these days Marshall protested the diaper-changing routine. He squirmed and kicked and gave his parents a hard time. But he seemed so surprised to have his sister inside the crib and ready to change him that he forgot to protest. Elisa opened the fresh diaper and slid it under the old diaper. She pulled the soiled diaper off of her brother and cleaned him with the wipes. Then, remembering how her mother did it, she pulled out the tabs and attached them to the sides of the diaper. "All done," said Elisa, snapping shut Marshall's pajama bottoms.

It was tricky climbing out of the crib while holding the dirty diaper and the soiled wipes in one hand. But somehow Elisa managed to do it. "Okay, Marshie," she said to him, "now it's time to go to sleep."

She turned off the light and closed the door. She threw the soiled things in the bathroom wastebasket and remembered to wash her hands. Then she went back to the living room. The boys were setting up the board for another game of chess.

"Who won?" asked Elisa.

"Guess," said Eugene Spencer.

"You did," said Elisa.

"Right."

"Why did you guess *him*? It could have been me," said Russell indignantly.

"But it wasn't," said Elisa. "Do you want to have the cookies now before you start the next game?"

"Sure," said Eugene Spencer. The three children went into the kitchen. They could still hear Marshall's voice coming from his bedroom. "Mamamama," he called.

"I think he wants a good-night hug and a kiss," said Elisa.

"Yuck," said Russell.

"My thought precisely," agreed Eugene Spencer.

"I'll go do it," said Elisa.

She went back to Marshall's room. She turned on the light and saw her little brother again standing in his crib. There were two pacifiers on the floor where they had fallen out between the bars of the crib. Or maybe Marshall had thrown them down. Elisa picked them up and put them into the crib.

"Mommy and Daddy went out," she told him. "I'll give you an extra kiss but then you have to go to sleep."

She tried to hug Marshall through the bars of the crib, but it was impossible. So she climbed back up and in once again. She put her arms around her brother. "Good-night, sweet dreams," she said, echoing the words her mother usually said to her. She kissed his soft cheek. "Now lie down," she told him.

Marshall lay down again. Elisa pulled up his blanket and covered him. She handed him his teddy bear and one of his pacifiers. "Go to sleep," she said as she climbed out of the crib.

Marshall looked at her and blinked. His mouth made the funny sucking sound that it always made when his pacifier was inside. Elisa turned off the light and closed the door. She walked back to the kitchen.

"We're finished eating," said Russell as he and Eugene Spencer left the kitchen. "We have to get back to playing chess."

Elisa went over to the counter. She picked up the box of cookies and shook it. The box felt very light. She put her hand inside and found one whole and one broken piece of cookie remaining. Elisa had a feeling that Russell had eaten a lot more than three cookies. But maybe not. Maybe Eugene Spencer had eaten them all. Elisa ate the broken piece first and then the whole one. The boys had left a few cookie crumbs on the kitchen counter. She ate them, too. She put the empty box in the garbage pail and the boys' glasses in the sink.

Then she went back into the living room.

The second chess game was already over. Elisa didn't have to ask who won. She could tell by her brother's unhappy face. "Are you going to play another game?" she asked.

"Sure," said Eugene Spencer. "I'm on a roll."

"No, I'm tired of chess," said Russell. "Let's watch TV."

"That's fine with me," said Eugene Spencer. The boys went to turn on the television. Elisa picked up the chess pieces and put them in their box. Then she went and sat down at the end of the sofa. Her library book was on the floor where one of the boys had thrown it. She picked it up and put it on the coffee table. Then she sat down again. The boys were looking at something with lots of shooting and yelling. It would have been fun to sit with them, but Elisa didn't like such gunny programs. She took her library book and went into her bedroom. Then she changed into her pajamas and got into bed. Elisa opened her book and began reading. But as she read, she could hear that Marshall was still awake. He wasn't talking or singing anymore. Now he was shaking his crib and shouting, "Mamamama!"

Elisa knew that on nights when he did this, her mother always went into his room to make him lie down. She put her bookmark in the book to save her page and went to Marshall's room. Sure enough, her brother was standing up and holding onto the side of his bed.

"Mamamama," he called out when he saw

his sister. He began to cry for his mother.

"I told you that Mommy went out," Elisa said. "But you know she always comes home to us."

Marshall kept on crying. Elisa listened to hear if Eugene Spencer would come and help out. But all she heard was the sound of the television movie. "Don't cry, Marshie," she said. "I'll sing you a song."

Elisa climbed back up into her brother's crib. "Come on," she told him. "Lie down and I'll lie next to you."

Marshall lay down. Elisa pushed one of his stuffed toys out of the way to make a space for herself. "*I love you. You love me. We're a happy family. . . .*'" She sang softly. Marshall sang along with her. She sang all the way to the end of the song and began singing it again. Then she sang it another time.

"Elisa? There you are! What are you

doing in here?" asked her father. "We were looking for you."

"It seems we have two babies in this crib," said Mrs. Michaels, laughing.

Elisa opened her eyes. She looked around and discovered that she was inside Marshall's crib.

"I'm not a baby," she said, responding to her mother's words. "I came to sing a song to Marshie," she remembered. "He didn't want to go to sleep." She looked at her little brother, who was so soundly asleep now that neither the light nor the voices were waking him up.

"I'm sorry that we woke you," said her mother, "but you'll be much more comfortable in your own bed. Tell me, how was Eugene Spencer as a baby-sitter?"

"I don't know," Elisa replied, sitting up in the crib. "He didn't do anything."

"Of course not," said Mr. Michaels,

nodding. "Baby-sitting is very easy work. Go to bed now," he told his daughter as he helped her climb down to the floor. "Before you know it, you'll be old enough to be working as a baby-sitter yourself."

"Yes," said Elisa, yawning as she walked back to her bedroom. "I've already had lots of practice," she called to her parents.

What Marshall Needed

Suddenly Marshall wasn't a baby anymore. He was walking. He was talking. He was feeding himself and he was able to play games with Elisa.

"Marshall is a real person these days," said Mrs. Michaels proudly.

"That's silly," said Russell. "Marshall was always a real person. But he's still a baby in my book."

"Babies crawl," said Elisa. "Marshall doesn't crawl anymore. He walks just like we do."

"Yeah, well, how about school? Marshall doesn't have to go to school, the lucky duck," Russell retorted.

"Oh, Russell. You always complain about school. But I know you like it. You have so many good friends there and you're always learning new and interesting things," said his mother.

"Well, sometimes I like school. It's fun working with computers, and I love phys ed," Russell admitted. "But Marshall doesn't go to school. So he's still a baby."

"He doesn't go to school, but he has a play group," pointed out their mother. "He plays with other children three mornings a week. That's the way you began, too: play group, preschool, kindergarten, and then first grade. Before you know it, Marshall will be in first grade and away at school all day long."

"But I won't be in second grade then," said Elisa. She tried counting on her fingers to figure out what grade she'd be in when Marshall reached first.

"Yeah, well, what about his diapers?" asked Russell. "Marshall still wears diapers. That proves he's a baby."

Mrs. Michaels nodded. "That's true. He does still wear diapers. But so did you when you were two years old. Give him a little more time and the diapers will be gone."

"What about his packy?" asked Elisa. "Nobody has one of those. Even in preschool, no one had a packy."

Elisa was referring to the pacifier that Marshall was forever sucking on. It had begun when he was an infant. He cried and fussed a great deal. He wasn't hungry. He didn't have gas. He wasn't tired. He was just unhappy and unable to let anyone know what his problem was. It was Nana who had suggested that he needed a pacifier. And it worked. In fact, it worked so well that soon their mother had bought half a dozen. If one pacifier fell on the ground when she was taking Marshall for his walk, she could immediately give him a clean one and put the other in her purse to be washed back home.

When Marshall went to sleep at night, he always had a pacifier in his mouth and three or four others in his crib with him. That way if he lost one in the night, or if one slipped through the bars of the crib, there was always a supply of those little nipples mounted on a piece of plastic waiting for him. He was a much happier infant after he had been introduced to the pacifier. And he didn't seem to want to outgrow this need.

In fact, it was rare to see Marshall without

the pacifier in his mouth.

"He's still a baby," said Russell, "but even so, he's too big for that thing in his mouth."

"Marshall, give me your packy," Elisa sometimes cooed to her little brother when they were playing. Marshall good-naturedly took it from his mouth and gave it to her. But a minute later he demanded to have it back.

"You're too big for a pacifier," said Elisa.

"I need it," said Marshall.

"Only little babies have pacifiers," said his mother.

"I need it," insisted Marshall.

He took the pacifier from Elisa and went looking for his others. He lined them up in a row and counted. "One-two-three-four-five packies," he reported proudly.

"A boy who's smart enough to count doesn't need a pacifier," said Mrs. Michaels.

"Red, green, blue, yellow, white," Marshall

said, pointing to the colored disks on which the pacifiers were mounted.

"A kid who knows colors is too big for a pacifier," said Russell.

"I need it," Marshall told him.

So there he was, getting bigger, getting smarter, but still sucking on his pacifier every day and all night long, too.

One autumn Saturday, when the weather was particularly sunny, Mr. Michaels suggested that the whole family go to the zoo. It was one of those rare Saturdays when neither Russell nor Elisa had a play date. "It's a long time since we all went on an outing together," their father said.

"Yeah. But I'm too old for the zoo," said Russell. "So I think I'll stay home."

"How can you be too old for the zoo?" asked his mother. "I remember how you always loved going there when you were young. And you're still younger than your

father and I. We don't have any objections to going to the zoo."

"It's different for you," Russell tried explaining. "You're parents. So you have to go places and do things like that. But I don't."

"You're not a parent, but you're a big brother," Mr. Michaels pointed out. "You can help me keep an eye on Marshall. Besides," he added, "it's just possible that before the weekend is out I'll take you to see that new movie, *Strange Creatures from the Lagoon.* How about it?"

"Is that a bribe?" asked Russell.

"What's a bribe?" asked Elisa.

"Absolutely not," said his father. "I wouldn't think of offering you a bribe. I'm just encouraging you to be part of this family outing."

"I'm going to be a bribe when I grow up," said Elisa. "And I'll wear a long, long white dress."

"In the meantime, get your jacket," said her mother.

Everyone put on their jackets and caps.

"Zoo, zoo," crowed Marshall happily. He loved going to the zoo.

"What will we see there?" asked his mother.

"Elephants, giraffes, seals, bears, monkeys."

"Smart boy," she said, smiling at him.

"Packy!" shouted Marshall as they headed for the door.

"What kind of animal is that?" joked Mr. Michaels.

Marshall didn't think it was a joke. "Packy. I need my packy."

Mrs. Michaels gathered up all of her son's pacifiers, and Marshall stuffed one in his mouth.

"You're too big for that pacifier," Russell told Marshall as they left their apartment.

Marshall removed it so that he could

speak. "I need it," he reminded his brother. Then he put the pacifier back into his mouth.

There were many families at the zoo. And there were lots of animal families inside the cages. The Michaelses saw the newborn elephant baby standing with her parents. They saw the lion cubs with their parents. And they watched a small giraffe trying to reach the high tree branches like her parents.

Then they got to the gorilla cage. A new baby gorilla was inside. He lay in his mother's arms as she was grooming him. He held on to his mother's hair as they swung from a tree branch.

"You know what that baby gorilla needs?" asked Elisa.

Marshall removed the pacifier from his mouth to respond. "Banana?" he asked.

Elisa shook her head no.

"He needs a pacifier," said Elisa.

Russell let out a loud laugh and slapped Elisa on the back. "That's a good one," he said.

Marshall took the pacifier out of his mouth again. "Gorillas don't have pacifiers," he told his sister.

"That's because they don't know where to buy them," said Elisa. "I bet that gorilla wishes he had a packy. See how he's looking at you?"

Marshall stood staring at the baby gorilla.

"I know what," said Russell. "Why don't you give your pacifiers to him?"

"That's a good idea," Elisa agreed, smiling at her big brother.

Russell went over to one of the zoo attendants and spoke to him. Mr. Michaels raised his eyebrows, but he didn't say a word. Mrs. Michaels looked at Marshall, but she didn't say anything either.

Russell came back. "The zookeeper said you could give your pacifiers to the baby gorilla if you don't need them anymore."

Marshall took the pacifier out of his mouth and looked at it. He looked at the baby gorilla. Elisa could see that he was thinking. He put the pacifier back into his mouth. Then Marshall reached for his mother's canvas tote bag. He stuck his hand inside and found his red, green, yellow, and white pacifiers. He took the blue pacifier out of his mouth.

"I don't need them," he said. "I'm a big boy."

"Are you sure?" asked Elisa. She was amazed by Marshall's decision.

Marshall nodded and looked serious. "I'll give them to the gorilla," he told Russell.

"Let's give them to the zookeeper. He'll put them inside the cage for the baby gorilla," Russell suggested.

"Okay," said Marshall. "I'm a big boy," he told the man as he handed over his pacifiers.

"Thank you very much," the zoo attendant said to Marshall.

"Thank *you*," Mrs. Michaels told the man.

"Let's go to the cafeteria and buy some lunch," suggested Mr. Michaels.

Marshall called out the names of all the animals they passed along the way to the cafeteria. It was easier for him to speak without having the pacifier in his mouth.

They had hot dogs and french fries and fruit punch to drink. Marshall used a cup just like the others now that he was a big boy. He only spilled a very little bit.

On the way home they stopped in the gift shop. Russell picked out a magnifying glass that came in a little leather case. Elisa found a tiny teddy bear that would be just the right size as a toy for her doll Airmail back home. And Marshall, who was becoming fascinated by dinosaurs, found himself a plastic one.

"It's a styracosaurus," he announced proudly.

No one said it, but everyone in his family had the same thought. A boy who could recognize a styracosaurus and say its name was certainly too old for a pacifier.

Chocolate All Day Long

"You know what my favorite thing is?" Elisa asked one night as she was going to bed.

"Me?" asked her mother, giving her a hug.

"No," said Elisa, giggling. "My favorite thing to eat. Not my favorite person."

"Spaghetti and meatballs?" asked Russell, looking up from the book he was reading for his class book report.

"Better than spaghetti," said Elisa.

"Pizza?" asked her father.

"Better than pizza," said Elisa.

"The best thing would be if you'd go to bed," said Russell. "I'm trying to concentrate."

"Russell, that's not nice," scolded his father.

"Oh, Dad, Elisa knows I'm just teasing," said Russell, giving his sister a wink.

Elisa attempted to wink back, but she still found it hard to do. Both her eyes closed whenever she tried.

"Okay, Elisa, we all give up. What's your favorite food?" asked Mr. Michaels.

"Chocolate," said Elisa.

"Well, isn't that interesting," said Mr. Michaels. "It so happens that I know where there is a piece." He walked into the kitchen and returned with a small square of chocolate, which he presented to his daughter. "Just be sure you brush your teeth again," he told her.

"No fair," Russell called out. "I want some chocolate too."

"Russell, you said you weren't interested in this conversation," his father reminded him.

"But I'm interested in chocolate," complained Russell.

"Then isn't it lucky that I found *two* pieces," remarked Mr. Michaels, showing his other hand.

"I love chocolate," said Elisa. "I could eat it all day long."

"It would make you sick," said Russell, licking the chocolate off his fingers.

"No it wouldn't," said Elisa.

"You'd get sick of it," said her mother.

"No I wouldn't," said Elisa. "I'd never get sick of chocolate."

"Bedtime," said Mrs. Michaels. "Go brush your teeth and into bed, quickly," she told her daughter.

"If I could have one wish in all the world,

I'd wish to eat only chocolate," said Elisa. She thought for a minute. "Saturday is my half birthday," Elisa reminded her mother. "Could I have chocolate all day long?"

"Isn't Annie Chu coming for a sleepover on Friday?" asked Mrs. Michaels. "She might not want to eat chocolate all day long. And I don't know how her mother would feel about it, anyway. It's not a very healthy diet."

"Well, Annie is coming after supper on Friday, and she'll only be at our house for breakfast on Saturday. So she could have a chocolate breakfast if she wanted or she could eat regular, boring stuff."

"Yeah, like French toast," said Russell. "Or waffles. They're not chocolate, but they're awfully good. And they're not boring either."

"All right," Mrs. Michaels told Elisa. "For your half birthday you can have chocolate all day long."

"I can't believe it," said Russell. "You're really going to let her get away with it?"

"I've had a lot of practice letting my children get away with things," said his mother. "Starting with you."

"Never," insisted Russell. "I never had chocolate all day long."

"True. But you had other things."

So that's why, when Elisa and Annie Chu woke up on Saturday morning, there was hot cocoa waiting for them in the kitchen. There was also a platter of waffles and sausages sitting on the middle of the table.

Russell was already eating one of the waffles. "These are great," he said.

"Oh, I love waffles," said Annie as she sat down. "I never get them at my house."

Elisa reached over to help herself to one of the waffles.

"Sorry, honey. They aren't made of chocolate," pointed out her mother. "But here's a mug of hot cocoa for you."

Elisa watched as Annie drank down a glass of orange juice. Then she sat looking as her friend took a waffle and two little sausages for her breakfast. Annie poured maple syrup on the waffle. It looked good. But it wasn't as good as chocolate. Elisa knew that for certain.

"What can I eat that's chocolate?" Elisa asked her mother.

Mrs. Michaels thought for a minute. "Not waffles, not toast, not cereal, not eggs, not fruit. Oh, I know," she said, and went to the cupboard. She returned holding two chocolate cookies in her hand. "These are chocolate," she said.

"Cookies for breakfast?" asked Annie. "I never heard of that."

"That's nothing. Elisa says she's going to eat only chocolate all day today," said Mrs. Michaels.

"I like chocolate," said Annie. "But I like lots of other things."

Elisa smiled smugly and munched on her chocolate cookies. The waffles smelled good. The sausages smelled good. She knew that they probably tasted pretty good, too. But she didn't want them today. She finished her mug of hot cocoa and asked for seconds.

When breakfast was over, the two girls had just enough time to draw with Elisa's new markers before her friend's mother came to pick Annie up. Since the night before when Annie had arrived, they had played Dress Up, Princess, School, and done two jigsaw puzzles together. They had watched Russell perform some magic tricks that he'd been learning from a kit he'd gotten for his birthday, and they'd played Zoo, crawling on the floor and pretending to be animals with Marshall.

After Annie went home, Mrs. Michaels

bundled Marshall into some warm clothing so they could go to the supermarket.

"Wait for me," said Elisa. "I want to go with you."

"No. You stay here with Daddy and Russell," said her mother. "You have a lot of cleanup to do."

Elisa made a face. It had been fun playing all those games with Annie, but it wouldn't be so much fun putting all the dress-up costumes back in their box and sorting out the markers, books, papers, puzzle pieces, and other things into their proper places.

"What are you going to buy?" Elisa asked.

"Groceries mostly. But I have to stop at the drugstore, too," said her mother as she and Marshall left the apartment.

Elisa felt hungry. She hadn't eaten very much for breakfast. She wondered if there were any waffles left over. She went into the kitchen, where she found her father drinking a cup of coffee and talking with Russell.

"Looking for some chocolate?" Russell asked.

"No. I just want a drink of water."

"I don't think our water is chocolate-flavored. You shouldn't have any today if you're only going to eat chocolate," Russell teased.

"Water is fine," said Mr. Michaels. "Help yourself," he told Elisa. So she drank a glass of water. It wasn't very satisfying. It would be much more interesting if chocolate-flavored water flowed out of the faucet.

Elisa went and slowly cleaned up all the mess in her bedroom. She decided that the next time Annie or one of her other friends came to visit, she wouldn't let them go home until they helped her with the cleanup. It was only fair, she thought. She heard her mother's key in the lock. Goody, she thought. Soon we'll be having lunch.

Lunch was vegetable soup and grilled cheese sandwiches. Elisa could smell them cooking all the way in her bedroom. But she remembered that she was having chocolate. She wondered what her mother was giving her. When she went into the kitchen, she saw. There at her place was a chocolate bar and a glass of chocolate milk. She wouldn't have objected to eating a bowl of soup and a sandwich first. Then she could have eaten the chocolate bar for dessert. But she certainly wasn't going to give Russell the satisfaction of knowing that.

"Goody. More chocolate for me," she said, ripping the wrapper off the bar. She broke the bar into pieces and ate them one after the other. She tried to ignore the aroma of the soup and the grilled cheese. The chocolate tasted good but not quite as good as usual. It probably would have

tasted better with plain milk instead of chocolate milk, Elisa realized.

"Anyone want another half sandwich?" offered Mrs. Michaels.

Russell did. Marshall was still chewing away on his first half. "Do elephants have taste bugs?" he asked.

"I think all creatures have taste buds," Mr. Michaels said. "But I don't know for sure. I'll look it up on the Internet later."

"Taste bugs. That's a good one." Russell laughed.

Elisa's taste buds or taste bugs were complaining inside of her. She could imagine the taste and texture of a grilled cheese sandwich.

"Look what I fixed for dessert," said Mrs. Michaels, opening the refrigerator.

"Dessert?" asked Russell. They didn't usually have dessert at lunchtime.

"Chocolate pudding. Since it's Elisa's half

birthday and she's eating only chocolate today, I thought it would be nice if we could all have the same thing."

Elisa loved chocolate pudding. She stuck her spoon in and helped herself to a large mouthful. The pudding was finished one-two-three.

"What's for supper tonight?" asked Elisa.

"Supper? I haven't even cleared the table from lunch," said Mrs. Michaels. "Besides, whatever it is, you won't be eating it. I have another chocolate bar for your supper. And maybe some chocolate ice cream for dessert."

"Oh," said Elisa. "That's good." But it wasn't. Her stomach was still hungry, and now she had to wait until suppertime to eat her next meal.

One of Russell's classmates, Philip, came over during the afternoon. The two boys were going to play chess together. Elisa stood watching until Russell made her go away.

"I can't concentrate with you standing there breathing on me," he complained.

"Well, I have to breathe," said Elisa. "Everyone does."

"Yes. But you don't have to stand right here. Go away."

Suddenly, Elisa smelled something familiar. Russell looked up from the chessboard and grinned at Philip. "Popcorn," he said.

"Oh, good," said Philip.

Elisa smiled at the thought of a mouthful of salty, buttery popcorn until she remembered. Popcorn wasn't made of chocolate.

She walked into her bedroom and sat down on her bed. She'd been hungry before, but the smell of the popcorn made her feel hungrier still. She didn't think she'd be able to survive until tomorrow morning when it wasn't her half birthday any longer and she could eat regular food like soup and sandwiches and fruit and juice and all the other things that people usually ate. If only Russell wouldn't tease her, she could have told her mother that she'd changed her mind. But Elisa absolutely refused to let Russell win an argument. And she could just imagine how he would act.

Elisa closed her bedroom door to block out the aroma of the popcorn. She drew some pictures with her box of pastels. When Marshall woke from his afternoon nap, she joined him in the living room and helped him build with his blocks. Unfortunately, even though Russell and Philip had eaten all the popcorn, the whole apartment still smelled of it. So all the while Elisa was playing with Marshall, her stomach was grumbling angrily inside her.

Marshall drank some juice and had some animal crackers for an afternoon snack. Elisa wondered if she could sneak one of the little animal crackers into her mouth. Just as she was about to reach for a cookie shaped like a tiger, the phone rang. Elisa jumped and took her hand away from the cookie. She heard her mother speaking on the phone.

The call was from Philip's mother. Their family was going to a Chinese restaurant for supper, and Russell had been invited to join them.

"This was a great afternoon," Russell said as he zipped his jacket shut. "Philip beat me three times and I beat him four. And now we're going out for supper."

"Come again, Philip," Mrs. Michaels called to their visitor. "Enjoy your meal, boys," she told them both.

The boys left and Mrs. Michaels went

into the kitchen. Mr. Michaels, who had gone to the gym, returned home. "Hmmm, something smells good," he called out as he entered the apartment. Elisa had already smelled it. Hamburgers!

She went into the kitchen. She counted four hamburgers cooking in the skillet on the stove. One for each of her parents, a small one for Marshall, and one more for Russell. Only Russell wasn't home, so there would be an extra one now.

"Could I have a hamburger for supper?" Elisa asked softly.

Mrs. Michaels looked up from the stove. "It's not chocolate," she pointed out.

"I know," agreed Elisa. "But it smells so good."

"That's because it *is* good," her mother said. "But there's no reason to stick to chocolate all day long if you want to eat a hamburger. Especially when we have an extra hamburger all ready to be eaten."

"It's not good to waste food," Elisa pointed out.

So Elisa helped out by having a hamburger on a bun with sliced tomatoes and pickles, french-fried potatoes, and half a grapefruit for dessert. It all tasted wonderful. It occurred to her that if Russell had been home, he would have insisted that she substitute chocolate syrup for the ketchup that she poured on her hamburger and potatoes.

Mr. Michaels had stopped at the public library and brought home a video for the family to watch after Marshall went to sleep. So when Russell returned home, they all saw *Babe*.

"This is a kiddie film," Russell complained before he sat back to enjoy it.

"No it's not," said Elisa. She had celebrated her half birthday and was feeling quite grown up. She had learned a lesson today and, best of all, Russell didn't even know it. Never again would she ask for chocolate all day long.

Marshall Makes Mischief

Every Friday afternoon Mrs. Michaels took her children to the public library. Now that he was so grown up, Russell was often too busy to join his younger brother and sister. But Elisa always looked forward to the outing. She was proud that she'd become a good reader and could understand chapter books. She always picked out two or three to borrow. But she also liked sitting in one of the beanbag chairs in the children's room and looking at picture books. She reread her old favorites and helped her mother select ones for Marshall.

Marshall liked going to the library, too. There were toys and other children that he could play with. Friday afternoon was always special for both Elisa and Marshall.

On the first Friday of December, the children's room was crowded as always, with children sitting at tables doing their homework together and others walking about selecting books or getting assistance from the two librarians. Elisa didn't remember their names, but one librarian was tall and had white hair and the other was short with black hair. That Friday, there was something extra in the children's room.

"A tree! A tree!" Marshall shouted gleefully. It wasn't a usual sight in the library.

Sure enough, in the center of the room

stood a large Christmas tree hung with decorations.

"It's beautiful," Elisa said, rushing to get a closer look. The ornaments on the tree were fun to look at.

"Happy birthday!" shouted Marshall, pointing to the foot of the tree.

There on the floor, surrounding the tree, were several gift-wrapped parcels. Elisa bent over and picked one up. Considering the size of the package, it felt very light. She shook the box, but nothing rattled inside. A gift tag attached to the package read *For King Babar from Queen Celeste*. She took the present over to the desk where the dark-haired children's librarian was sitting. "Is this really for King Babar?" Elisa asked. "Will he come here to get his present?"

The librarian laughed. "One of the librarians on our staff thought this would be a good joke. But it seems to confuse people more than anything. The packages are all empty, but the gift cards are a reminder of some of the characters you may have met in your library books." The librarian smiled at Elisa. "Would you please put that package back under the tree for me?"

"Oh," said Elisa with a twinge of disappointment. She hadn't really thought there was an elephant king named Babar, but it would have been wonderful if she was wrong. She returned the package to its place under the tree and looked at some of the others. She was pleased that at least she could read all the labels:

For Mr. McGregor from Peter Rabbit
For Baby Bear from Goldilocks
For Grandmother from Little Red Riding Hood.

Mrs. Michaels came over to Elisa. "Do you think you are old enough to keep an eye on Marshall for just a couple of minutes?

There's a book I want to look for downstairs in the adult section of the library."

"Yes. Yes," said Elisa, proud to be given that job. "Where is Marshie?" she asked, looking around for her little brother.

"He's over in the preschool area playing with the blocks."

Elisa looked and saw Marshall with half a dozen other little children nearby. There were several parents standing about or sitting at the very small tables in the preschool area, too. The parents were all busy talking with one another.

"Okay," said Elisa. "I'll look for my books when you come back." She went over to the preschool section and sat down at one of the tables. She could remember when that very table and its chair had seemed large to her.

Marshall was making a tower. Six blocks in front of him were piled one on top of another. Elisa watched as Marshall carefully put a seventh block onto the pile. The pile began to wobble. "It's going to fall over," she warned her brother.

"No it won't," said Marshall.

"Yes it will. Look how it's shaking," Elisa pointed out.

Marshall took another block, and before he could even place it on top of the stack, the whole thing fell down.

"See. I told you it was going to fall," Elisa said.

Usually, if the blocks fell when Marshall was building, he would start over again. And again. He seemed to like the crash that he caused as much as the act of building. But today Marshall turned his back on the blocks. He ran toward the Christmas tree. "Tree, tree," he called out cheerfully.

Elisa rushed after him.

"Happy birthday!" Marshall shouted, grabbing one of the packages.

"Put it back," said Elisa. "The librarian said she wants all the packages under the tree."

"It's mine," said Marshall, holding tightly to the package.

"No it's not," said Elisa. She decided that it would be better not to grab it from her brother. If she did, he might begin howling. So instead she spoke softly, the way her mother did. "Marshall, that's not a real present," she explained. "It's only an empty box."

"No. No," said Marshall. "Happy birthday." It wasn't so long since he had celebrated his birthday, and he still remembered all the gift-wrapped packages he had received.

"Marshall, come with me," said Elisa, reaching for her brother's hand. "I'll help you make a new tower."

"No, no," said Marshall, running away and still holding the package. Elisa rushed after him. Marshall ran past the librarian's desk and past the children's computer area. He ran into one of the rows of shelves where the chapter books were kept.

When Elisa caught up with him, he had already pulled off the ribbon and was ripping the colorful gift wrap from the package. "Happy birthday!" Marshall said gleefully as he tried to pry open the box.

"Oh, no, Marshie!" shrieked Elisa in dismay. She was in charge of her brother, and in one minute he had done something terrible.

Marshall pulled the lid from the cardboard box. Inside there was some tissue paper. He tore at it, searching for whatever toy it hid, but there was no toy at all. Elisa looked around. Luckily there weren't any children searching for books in the aisle where she and Marshall were standing. She grabbed the ribbon and the gift wrap and stuffed them behind some books on the shelf. Then she squashed the box as flat as she could and put it and the tissue paper behind some books, too. Maybe no one would notice that Mr. McGregor's package was missing.

"Don't do that again," she said, turning around to look at Marshall. But he wasn't there. She knew exactly where he had gone. Sure enough, when she hurried back to the Christmas tree, there was Marshall, about to rip open another package.

"Marshall. Stop that!" she shouted at him, and ran to grab the package away.

"No. It's mine," Marshall yelled back at her.

"Marshall. Do you need a time-out?" Elisa screamed, pulling the package from him.

"No. No."

"You're in big trouble," Elisa yelled.

"No. No. It's mine," Marshall cried out. He got down on the floor and kicked his feet in anger. Luckily there was carpeting on the floor so it wasn't as noisy as when he kicked his feet at home. Then he ran to the tree and grabbed another package.

"Please," a voice called, "there's no shouting in the library."

"I can't help it," said Elisa, starting to cry. "He's not listening to me. I'm watching him and he keeps doing bad things."

"Oh, honey, don't cry," said the dark-haired librarian, smiling at Elisa. She crouched down to Marshall's level. "Those are not real presents," she explained gently, taking the package from him. "It's just pretend."

"It's mine. Mine," shrieked Marshall, trying to pull the package away from the librarian.

"See what I mean," said Elisa, but her voice was drowned out by the shouts of other children.

"Mine. Mine," shouted another little boy

who had come to see what all the excitement was about.

"I want a present, too," shouted a little girl.

"Me too," said a boy, as he pulled a package from under the tree.

"How about everyone listening to a good story," the white-haired librarian called over the cries of all the children.

"I don't want a story. I want a present,"

the little girl shouted.

"Me too."

In the midst of all the children calling out for presents, Marshall ran off again. Elisa raced after him. He went back to the same aisle where he'd opened Mr. McGregor's package.

"Happy birthday?" he asked Elisa. He seemed to remember the package but had forgotten that it was empty.

"Look," said Elisa, pulling out books until she could locate the flattened box from the back of the shelf. "See, it was only a box. There was nothing inside."

At that moment the short librarian with dark hair came by. "Did you open one of our packages and hide it here?" she asked Elisa.

"Not me. I mean, I didn't *open* the package. My brother did. But I did hide it," Elisa admitted. "I didn't want him to get into trouble."

"Did you do that?" the librarian asked Marshall.

Marshall looked at her. "Happy birthday," he said.

"Is today your birthday?" the librarian wanted to know. "You're getting to be a big boy. How old are you now?"

"It's not his birthday," Elisa said angrily as Marshall proudly held up two fingers.

Just then a hand rested on Elisa's shoulder.

She looked up and saw her mother standing there. "What's going on?" Mrs. Michaels asked.

"Marshall wanted a present. He took one of the packages from under the tree," Elisa explained.

"It seemed like such a lovely idea," the librarian said, shrugging her shoulders. "But we'll never do it again. It's too tempting for the children to see what they think are presents waiting here for them."

"Library books are presents," said Mrs. Michaels firmly. "They're presents from the library for the borrowers."

"Exactly," said the librarian. "That's very well put."

"Come, Marshall," said Mrs. Michaels, taking her little son's hand. "Let's see if there's a new Spot book today."

"I don't want Spot," Marshall said angrily. "I want a present."

"How about a Curious George book, then?"

"No," said Marshall, shaking his head.

"Then what do you want?"

"Clifford."

"Well, let's go check the shelves," Mrs. Michaels said.

When Elisa went and looked under the tree again, all the packages had disappeared. It had been silly anyhow, she thought. Everyone knew that Mr. McGregor and King Babar and Goldilocks were only in stories. They wouldn't get presents. Elisa walked over to the fiction section and started looking for some good books to take home. As she reached for a book, she noticed some colored gift wrap stuck in the shelf. She gave a pull and it came out. There was a little tag attached to the paper. *For Harry Potter from Hermione*, it said. It looked as if Marshall wasn't the only child who had opened a package that wasn't addressed to him. But after all, Marshall didn't know how to read yet, so how could he know?

Elisa picked out three books. They all looked very good. Marshall and his mother found two Clifford books and one about Harry the dirty dog. Marshall liked books about animals, especially dogs and dinosaurs.

Walking home, holding her new library books, Elisa felt eager to read them. She'd start the first one tonight after supper. It was like having a new present to open, she thought. Her mother had been right about that.

From Riverside to Lakeside

Suddenly there were a hundred phone calls.

"Not a hundred," said Russell. "Don't exaggerate."

"Well loads and loads," said Elisa. She should have counted from the beginning. But she hadn't known it was the beginning then.

First the mother of Russell's friend Philip phoned on the Monday after Thanksgiving. Russell was invited to join Philip and his parents on a ski trip to Vermont. They would be away for a whole week during the winter break from school.

"I'll have to get back to you on that," Mrs. Michaels said. She wanted to discuss the trip with Russell and his father.

"You have to let me go," Russell insisted. "I've never gone skiing. It's the chance of a lifetime."

"Let me think about it," said his mother.

"I went away to camp. That was for *three* weeks. This is only *one*. So I won't get homesick. And Philip and I will have a great time. I've always wanted to go skiing."

"I never heard you talk about skiing," said Elisa.

"I never said it out loud, but I was thinking about it for a long time," Russell insisted. "Philip's parents are going to Vermont," Russell added. "I always wanted to go to Vermont. Please. Please."

Russell's parents discussed the ski trip with each other and with Philip's parents. In the end, they agreed that Russell could go.

"Y-E-S!" shouted Russell. He was thrilled and leaped all around their apartment. Marshall jumped around with Russell even though he wasn't going anywhere. Marshall didn't even know what skiing was. No one went skiing in Riverside Park.

Mrs. Michaels phoned Philip's parents and began making arrangements. Russell called Philip and learned all about his friend's ski trip the year before. Then Philip's mother phoned with a suggested list of things that Russell should bring along on the trip.

In the midst of all the calls about the skiing, the children's grandmother phoned from Florida. Friends of hers, named Mr. and Mrs. Herman, were traveling from New York to Florida for a week. They were departing on the Friday after Christmas, and they offered to chaperone Russell and Elisa on the trip down and back.

"A visit to Grandma?" asked Elisa.

Her mother nodded. "Won't you and Daddy and Marshall come, too?" Elisa asked.

"No. Perhaps another time. But this invitation was just for you and Russell."

"But what about skiing?" Russell asked.

"Well, you can't go to both places at once," said Mrs. Michaels. "But I'm sure that Philip and his parents will understand if you want to visit with your grandmother."

"Will we go on an airplane?" Elisa asked. That was how her grandmother traveled when she came to visit her. Elisa didn't know if she should be feeling happy or scared at this unexpected development.

"I always wanted to go on an airplane," said Russell.

"Can't Grandma come here to us?" suggested Elisa. That would be a much easier way to see her grandmother. She could sleep in her own bed and not have to leave her parents behind.

"Yeah," agreed Russell. "That's a good idea. Tell her to come here. Then I could go skiing and still get to see her. And then next time, we'll go visit her in Florida."

"You want to have your cake and to eat it, too," said his mother, nodding.

"What cake?" asked Elisa.

"Well, I promised Philip I'd go with him," said Russell. "Besides, that way Grandma could see the whole family and not just me and Elisa."

"What cake?" asked Elisa, still puzzled by what her mother had said.

"Well. We're not going to make any decisions just now," said Mrs. Michaels.

"Why didn't Grandma call sooner?" Russell complained. "Then I would have told Philip that I couldn't go with him." He paused for a moment. "The only trouble is that I do want to go with him. Why is life so complicated?"

It took many more phone calls to their grandmother, the Hermans, and to Philip's parents, too, until everything was worked out. In the end, Russell was still going skiing with Philip. And Elisa was going to travel with Mr. and Mrs. Herman when they flew down to Florida.

"Lucky duck," said Russell.

"You could be a lucky duck, too," Elisa reminded him.

"I am lucky. I'm going skiing," said Russell. "But I wish we were flying to Vermont and not going by car."

"I wish I was going by car and not flying," said Elisa. "I don't understand how an airplane can stay up in the air."

"By the engine," Russell explained.

"Oh," said Elisa. Then she wondered how

the engine knew to take the plane up in the air. Car engines kept cars down on the ground. She kept her mouth shut, but her mind kept on wondering.

Suddenly Christmas Day, a time that the children waited for all year long, didn't seem as important as usual. The day after Christmas, Russell was going skiing. And the following day, Elisa was flying to Florida. She wondered about Mr. and Mrs. Herman. She'd never even met them. It would be weird to travel with strangers.

Their mother helped the children pack their suitcases. Russell's suitcase was filled with warm clothing: sweaters, woolen socks, extra gloves, flannel shirts, and thick corduroy pants. The contents of Elisa's suitcase was just the opposite: sleeveless T-shirts and shorts, her bathing suit, and cotton summer dresses.

"Poor Marshie will be all alone," said Elisa.

"Not quite. Daddy and I will still be here," her mother pointed out.

Russell left, and the next day it was Elisa's turn. Her stomach felt funny, so she couldn't eat any breakfast.

"At least drink some juice," her mother urged her. "Maybe they'll give you something to eat on the airplane."

"How can you eat on an airplane?" Elisa asked.

"Exactly the same way that you eat on the ground," said her mother, laughing. "You put the food in your mouth and you chew and swallow."

Mr. Michaels took his daughter to the airport.

"How will we know who Mr. and Mrs. Herman are?" Elisa asked.

"We're going to meet at the ticket window. It's all arranged," her father reassured her. "I won't hand you over to the wrong people."

Sure enough, two tall, white-haired people were waiting for Elisa. They introduced themselves as Diane and Fred. Mr. Michaels shook their hands and spoke with them for a while. Then he hugged Elisa good-bye. Elisa concentrated hard so she wouldn't start crying. It was strange. On the one hand, she wanted so much to see her grandmother. On the other hand, she already missed the rest of her family. "Have a super time," her father said to her.

Elisa nodded but didn't say anything.

Luckily, going on an airplane involved enough new experiences that Elisa was kept too busy to cry. She had to walk through a doorway. Something began to beep as she did that.

"Step this way, young lady," said a man in a uniform. "Are you wearing any metal jewelry?" he asked her.

Elisa proudly held up her arm so the man

could see the beautiful charm bracelet she had gotten for Christmas from Nana, her other grandmother.

The man waved a black wand over the bracelet, and the beep went off again.

"Okay," the man said. "That's it."

They all went to sit in the waiting area. "This is our gate," Diane Herman told Elisa. Elisa couldn't see any gates. But she sat down on one of the seats next to the Hermans.

Many people were in the waiting area. Elisa was surprised to see that she wasn't the only child who was going to get on the plane. In fact, there seemed to be as many children as in her class at school—boys, girls, and babies. Some were sitting and some were running about. Some were silent and some were talking. Some of the babies were crying. Some were drinking and some were eating.

Elisa was carrying a tote bag that contained a chapter book and a book of puzzles. She also had Airmail, the rag doll that her grandmother had made for her a long time ago before she moved to Florida.

She was getting too big to play with dolls as much these days, but still it was comforting to have Airmail nearby. Besides, she thought, Airmail would enjoy seeing her grandmother again, and she had come in an airplane to get to Elisa in the first place.

"I'm going to get us some coffee," Fred Herman told Elisa. "Are you hungry?"

She shook her head no. But when he returned with a bag of doughnuts as well as the coffee for himself and his wife, Elisa accepted one. Her stomach was beginning to feel a little hungry after all. The doughnut had sugar sprinkled on it and it tasted good.

After a while there was an announcement about boarding the plane. Elisa held her tote bag in one hand and Mrs. Herman's hand with the other. They entered the plane, and an attendant smiled at Elisa. "Welcome aboard," she said.

Elisa smiled back. She saw that there were three seats on each side of a long aisle.

"We're in row seven," said Mr. Herman as they walked.

"Seven. Just like I'm seven," said Elisa.

"So you are," said Mrs. Herman, squeezing her hand.

"We're in seats D, E, and F."

"D, E, and F," Elisa said in amazement. "That stands for all our names: Diane, Elisa, and Fred."

"What a coincidence!" said Mrs. Herman, laughing.

They came to their seats and, after a moment's consideration, Elisa agreed that she really wanted to sit by the window, even though seat 7E was in the middle.

Elisa put her tote bag under the seat in front of her, as Mrs. Herman instructed.

Then she buckled her seat belt just as she did when she was in her parents' car. She looked out the window and could see the suitcases being loaded onto the plane. She tried to look everywhere and remember everything so she could report back to Russell.

A different airplane attendant smiled at Elisa. "Is this your first flight?" she asked her.

Elisa nodded.

A little later the attendant returned and gave Elisa a packet with stickers and a booklet to paste them in. There was also a pin of an airplane to attach to her sweater. Diane Herman helped Elisa put the pin on. "Don't you get one, too?" Elisa asked when she realized that she had been singled out for this treat.

"No. Only youngsters get these," Mrs. Herman answered.

When everyone was seated, the plane began moving slowly. Looking from the window, Elisa could see that they were passing the other planes that were nearby. The flight attendant recited some instructions, and Elisa tried to pay attention. But she was so busy looking out the window that she didn't hear everything. The plane began moving faster and faster on the ground. If her parents drove that quickly in their car, they would get a speeding ticket. But Elisa knew that airplanes were permitted to go so fast. Suddenly the ground tilted away from the window and Elisa realized that they were going up in the air.

"I'm flying!" she shouted in amazement.

Around her some people laughed at her excitement and surprise. But the Hermans understood how she felt. "Isn't it fun?" asked Mrs. Herman. Elisa nodded but didn't take her eyes from the window. She could see the shining water of the river below and the bridges and cars and houses getting smaller by the moment.

Even though she wanted to watch and remember everything, after a while there was nothing to see. "What's all this white stuff?" Elisa asked.

"Clouds," said Mr. Herman. "We're flying through them now."

"How will the pilot find his way?" Elisa asked. If they got lost, she wouldn't see her grandmother.

"It's all done by radar," said Mr. Herman. Elisa hadn't known she would fly through clouds. And when the plane rose above the clouds, she was amazed to see how blue the sky really was. They were too high to see anything but the clouds below them, but Elisa kept watching. She pressed her forehead against the cool window. The next thing she knew, Mrs. Herman was tapping her shoulder. "Wake up, Elisa, honey. We're here!"

"Here? We're in Florida?"

"Yep. You slept through almost the whole flight."

Well, not quite. They were still up in the air, but Elisa could see that the plane was on its way down. There was a funny feeling in her ears as she made out fields and trees, cars and people that were getting bigger by the moment. She looked to see if she could recognize her grandmother down below, but she couldn't. She wished her parents and Russell and Marshall would be there on the ground waiting for her, too.

At last the plane landed and Elisa could remove her seat belt. She picked up her tote bag with Airmail's head sticking out of it. Elisa followed Mr. Herman down the aisle with Mrs. Herman right behind her. They walked out the door and out of the plane. Amazing. Elisa had really flown. And Russell hadn't. She was a lucky duck, if only her family wasn't so far away.

And there waving to Elisa was her grandmother.

Elisa ran toward her and gave her a hug. Grandma hugged her back, and as she did Elisa suddenly remembered how good her grandmother always smelled. Like flowers growing in a garden.

"How tall you are!" her grandmother exclaimed. "I almost didn't recognize you."

"Yes you did," said Elisa, laughing. Her grandmother was making a joke.

"It's too bad that Russell couldn't come, too," Grandma said. "But we're going to be so busy that you won't have a chance to miss him. You'll be going swimming and walking on the beach. And there's an amusement park nearby and a wonderful art museum with special exhibitions for children."

They went to the baggage claim area and got Elisa's suitcase. She'd have to remember to tell Russell about how all the luggage went round and round, like a merry-go-round, but without music or horses going up and down, until each suitcase was claimed by its owner. Elisa said good-bye to Mr. and Mrs. Herman. She'd see them again when they all went back to New York together at the end of next week.

"A week is a long time," said Elisa sadly as she walked to her grandmother's car.

"It's long and it's short. I think this is going to be a short week. We'll be so busy having a good time that I'm afraid it's just going to fly."

"Like I just flew?" Elisa asked her grandmother.

"Exactly. It's going to fly so fast you won't have time to be homesick. I knit a new sweater for Airmail and I'm making a matching one for you. But I wanted to measure your arms, so I haven't finished it."

"Could you teach me to knit?" Elisa asked.

"What a great idea," said her grandmother. "That will be still another thing for us to do."

Everything her grandmother said sounded like fun. But something inside Elisa felt a little bit sad. "Grandma," she said.

"Yes, honey?"

"I miss Mommy and Daddy and Russell and Marshall." She hoped she didn't hurt her grandmother's feelings by saying that.

"That's wonderful," her grandmother replied.

"It is?" asked Elisa, wiping a tear that had suddenly dripped from underneath her eyeglasses.

"Of course it is. If you didn't miss them, I'd be very disappointed."

"You would?"

"Certainly. It means you love them. I always miss all of you whenever I fly back home here. But instead of being sad, I think about things I can do. That's why I made you Airmail and I knit you sweaters."

"Maybe I could knit a sweater for

Mommy," Elisa suggested.

"I don't think there will be enough time for that," said her grandmother. "But you could come with me to the yarn store and help me pick out the color you think your mother would like best. Then I'll knit her a sweater and it will come in the mail. It will be a surprise for her."

"And a secret!" said Elisa, smiling. "I won't tell."

"Good," replied her grandmother. "I'm getting hungry. Are you?"

Elisa nodded. Suddenly she was starving.

"Well, we're going straight home and having lunch," said her grandmother. "But I have a special plan for tomorrow morning. Guess what?"

Elisa shook her head.

"Tomorrow I'm going to make you those pancakes in the shape of animals like I used to make for your mother. And while you're eating them, I'll dial your home. You can have breakfast with your mom, just like you had breakfast with me. And you can tell her all about the things we do. How would you like that?"

"I'd like that a lot," Elisa said. And she did.